AGENT ARTHUR'S
ARCTIC
ADVENTURE

Martin Oliver

Illustrated by Paddy Mounter

Designed by David Gillingwater

Cover design: Russell Punter and David Gillingwater

Series editor: Gaby

TED SMART

D0227921

Contents

Arthur and the Action Agency

The Action Agency is a world wide undercover organization dedicated to fighting crime and solving mysteries. Supremely successful, the Agency lives up to its motto, *Search, Solve and Survive*, by operating a "go anywhere, do anything" service.

Arthur is the Agency's youngest recruit. His uncle is Jake Sharpe, the founder and brains of the Agency. He is an elusive figure and master of disguise.

Under Agency orders, Arthur and his canine companion Sleuth, are flying to Hudlum Bay in the Arctic Circle. Arthur is racking his brains, trying to remember vital Agency information, and not to think about holidays.

You can join Arthur's adventure by solving the puzzles that appear on almost every page. If you get stuck, you will find extra clues and all the answers at the back of the book.

A Munchy Message

A gent Arthur stepped out of the plane in Hudlum Bay, squinting as the sun glared off the snow. He glanced down at Sleuth who snorted in disgust at the blasts of icy wind, then growled at a nearby pack of huskies.

"Come on Sleuth," Arthur shouted. "Let's grab some food."

They slithered across the icy runway, down the main street and into a bar. Arthur quickly ordered, then looked around.

"Hudlum Bay seems normal enough," he thought, above the sound of Sleuth chomping. "I wonder why I was sent here?"

Arthur picked up his moose burger and took a huge bite. A piece of paper flew out of it. Arthur gasped as he spotted some familiar symbols. It was a message from the Action Agency!

What does the message say?

Making Contact

Arthur retrieved the key from under the iceberg lettuce. He gave Sleuth the note to dispose of, then paid the bill. Sleuth was chewing happily as they left the bar. Keeping alert for skidding skidoos and stray snowballs they headed out into the snowy streets.

Is the baked Alaska ready?

Y-y-yes. It'll be r-r-right on time.

They made it safely down Avalanche Avenue and across Polar Bear Boulevard. Arthur pushed open the post office door and strode inside. To his right he saw a row of telephones, and through a door he spotted the left-luggage lockers. Just then a phone began ringing. It was the green one!

Arthur dashed over to it and picked up the receiver. A muffled voice asked a familiar question. It was his contact. Arthur panicked for a second and wished Sleuth wasn't such a quick eater. Then he remembered what to say. He managed to stammer out his reply and waited.

Hello, this is Agent Alex. I'm in a safe house and have information about Spider Organization activities. We'll meet in the park. Hang on, there's a plane right overhead ... OK it's landed. Wait at the fountain SE of the safe house.

Ow!

Arthur listened intently to the agent. His brain reeled in shocked horror at the mention of the Spider Organization, the most powerful gang of criminals in the whole world and sworn enemies of the Action Agency.

Suddenly the voice broke off. Arthur strained his ears. He heard the sounds of a struggle. Then the line went dead.

Arthur stared at Sleuth in horror. A fellow Action Agent was in trouble. Arthur must race to his rescue, but where was Alex ? Sleuth barked and scampered off to the lockers. Arthur dashed after him and yanked open locker 13. The Essential Agency Kit fell out. Amongst the handy objects was a local town plan.

Where should Arthur go?

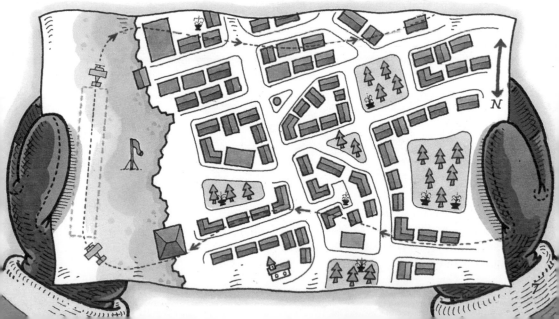

Arthur to the Rescue

Arthur's brain reeled for a second, then he sprang into action. Checking round to make sure no one was watching him, he quickly sorted through the Action Agency equipment and packed it into his rucksack.

Arthur grabbed the bag and chased after Sleuth who was racing for the door. They dashed outside, gasping for breath as the cold air hit them. Arthur stepped on a patch of black ice and skidded round a corner.

He careered across the street. Sleuth hardly dared watch as Arthur missed a skidoo and a startled shopper by inches.

As he struggled to stop his slippery slide, Arthur spotted a lamp post. He reached out and clung on desperately.

With Arthur treading carefully and keeping both eyes firmly on the ground, they reached their destination. Arthur studied the large timber house ahead.

"It all seems quiet enough," he whispered. "Maybe we've got the wrong place. I'll try Action Plan A, the direct approach."

He rang the bell and waited . . . and waited. Then he rang again.

At last the door creaked open and a spiky-haired woman stared out at him.

"I'm looking for Alex," Arthur said. "Does he live here?"

The reply seemed innocent enough, but as Arthur turned to go, he realized something was very wrong.

What is wrong?

Action Plan B

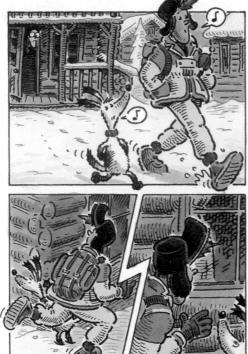

Arthur hastily mumbled an apology to the woman, then he and Sleuth walked nonchalantly away until they were out of sight of the house.

"Now for Action Plan B," Arthur hissed. "The sneaky approach."

Keeping to the shadows, they retraced their steps and crept round to the back of the house. Sleuth sniffed the air for danger. It was OK, no one had spotted them. Arthur heard voices inside the house, and, with all senses on red alert, peered in through a grubby window.

He saw the spiky–haired woman and the man from the upstairs window. Arthur's ears pricked up at what he overheard. He whispered a plan to Sleuth who scampered away to trail the burly man.

Who was that?

Just some pesky kid. You join the others with our new hostage, Agent Alex, back at base. I'll search for the information then get back to base. Arrange decoys to put any meddlers off my trail.

You follow the man. I'll watch the woman then tail her back to base. We'll meet there.

Arthur looked back into the room and gasped. The woman was methodically ransacking the room. As Arthur watched her closely he thought that she seemed vaguely familiar.

Arthur racked his brains while the woman carried on searching. She grew more and more angry, ripping up floorboards and checking papers and books, but to no avail. Eventually she vaulted out of the window empty handed, aimed a furious karate kick at a water barrel and hurried away.

Just then Arthur remembered a recent Action Agency file. Now he knew who the woman was, but that still left many questions unanswered. If only she had left something that might give Arthur a lead, but she had been too careful.

Or had she?

CROOKFAX
Name:
BELLA DONNA
Leader of the Trapper Gang - known links with notorious Spider Organization.

Seeing Doubles

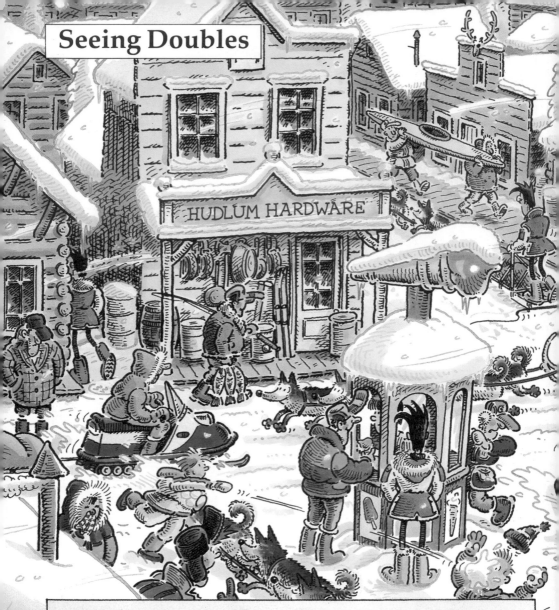

A rthur picked up the card. One side was blank, on the flip side were two strangely written words. But there was no time to guess what they meant. Bella was striding away and Arthur musn't lose sight of her.

Arthur raced down the street and into the busy town square. Arthur spotted a woman who looked like Bella. He was about to follow her when he saw another one . . . then another . . . and another.

They were all heading in different directions. Which one should he follow? If only Sleuth were there, he could have sniffed out the real villain from the decoys. But they all looked identical to Arthur.

He stared hard at the women, until in a flash he realized he could work out which one was the real Bella Donna.

Which figure should Arthur follow?

On the Trail

Arthur watched Bella leave the crowded square then he set off through the quiet alleys after her. Tiptoeing silently from building to building, he stalked his quarry through the backstreets of Hudlum Bay.

Arthur tried to melt into the background as his footsteps crunched over the snow. Up ahead Bella stopped. She seemed to be listening for something. Suddenly she whirled round brandishing a gun.

Halt, who goes there? What's the password?

Minutes later a dark, hairy bundle jumped up at Arthur. It was Sleuth. The two of them hid behind a crate and watched Bella walk up to a canning factory. This must be the crooks' base.

"We've got to get inside," Arthur whispered. "But how can we get past the guard?"

Just then the guard asked Bella for the password.

Arthur dived for cover and held his breath. He looked up. Bella was coming right at him. Just then a black cat darted out in front of Arthur. The villain smiled, lowered her revolver, turned and walked away.

As soon as Arthur's pulse rate returned to normal, he cautiously picked himself up, brushed himself down and started off again. Bella marched on quickly, unaware of the shadowy presence following her.

Pass boss. The rest are waiting inside.

It's me you dummy. OK, the password is . . . mumble . . . mutter.

Arthur couldn't hear her reply, but he noticed the guard checking a card identical to the one Bella had dropped. Arthur realized that the card must be a clue to the password.

As the guard let Bella in, Arthur stared at the card and stepped forwards. He was sure he knew the password.

What is the password?

The guard let them pass without a murmur and Arthur and Sleuth stepped confidently into the canning factory. They were inside the crooks' base!

Sleuth wrinkled his nose up at the awful smell, then led the way down a corridor and up some stairs. Arthur cautiously opened the door ahead and crept out on to a balcony. He ducked behind a packing case as Sleuth growled a warning.

"Something fishy's going on here," whispered Arthur as he peered down. "This must be the Trapper Gang."

Arthur glanced around at the strange assortment of people below. Agent Alex was nowhere to be seen, but Arthur spotted some familiar faces.

Who has Arthur recognized? Where has he seen them?

Spider Plans

W here was Agent Alex being held, and what devious plans were these gangsters hatching? Arthur decided to investigate further. Sleuth acted as listen-out while Arthur doubled back, snapped on his torch and crept stealthily down a dingy corridor. Up ahead was a door. Arthur stopped, everything seemed quiet. He was just about to try the lock when pain shot up his leg.

"Get off," Arthur hissed until he suddenly realized why Sleuth had stopped him.

Arthur ducked then limped quietly after Sleuth, who led him down another corridor and into an empty office. Sleuth pawed at a locked attache case.

Arthur fumbled with his Agency skeleton key. The lock sprang open. He spread out the contents of the case and stared excitedly at the photos, pictures and writing. Could these be the Spider Organization's plans? He had to decode them.

Can you decipher the codes?

19

Action Agent Alex

These plans were dynamite! Arthur's brain reeled as he snapped a photo with his Agency mini-camera. His mission now must be to find Ice Station Spider and stop the villains, but what about his contact, the kidnapped Action Agent?

Arthur bundled the plans back into the case. He left the office and began carefully searching the factory. Arthur inched his way down a corridor.

He had just turned left when he heard faint groaning sounds. Where had they come from?

"I don't know who made that noise," hissed Arthur sweeping the area with his torch. "But my Action Agent's Instinct tells me that they're in trouble."

Sleuth sniffed the air and wagged his tail. The groaning started again. Arthur stared at the pool of light ahead.

He spotted a figure propped up against a packing case. Arthur recognized his contact in Hudlum Bay. It was Action Agent Alex. He was bound and gagged.

Arthur knelt down and checked that the agent was OK. Alex's eyes opened wide in amazement when he saw Arthur. As Arthur gently peeled off the gag, Alex whispered a vitally important message. When Alex finished, Sleuth began biting through the ropes round his ankles, but the agent stopped him.

"Leave me here," he hissed. "Otherwise those villains will know they've been rumbled."

Arthur didn't want to leave his fellow agent in the crooks' clutches, but there was no time to argue. Just then Sleuth growled a warning. He could hear footsteps heading towards them. There was nowhere to run to. They must hide, and quickly.

Where can Arthur and Sleuth hide?

Arctic Supplies

Arthur held his breath as the footsteps approached . . . then passed by. Throughout the night he heard shouts and the sounds of things being pushed and dragged around.

It was light before the coast was clear. Arthur nudged Sleuth and they crept out of the case. They dashed out of the deserted factory and back into town. There was no time to lose in getting to the log cabin at Caribou Creek.

"But we can't head off into the icy Arctic wastes," Arthur said, shivering at the thought. "Not until we buy new gear and find Codename Snowstorm."

Arthur flicked through the Agency Handbook. He racked his brains to remember Survival Lesson E for Essential Arctic Equipment, while Sleuth led the way to the shops.

They carefully selected the thickest Arctic gear, and ten layers later they waddled out. Sleuth checked their food supplies while Arthur tested camping equipment.

They staggered out of the ski shop. Arthur hired a souped-up skidoo, test drove it to the garage and filled up the tank and the spare petrol cans.

Last of all Arthur bought a sturdy radio. Now they were ready to go, except for one thing; they still hadn't found the undercover Action Agent in town. Arthur thought back to what he had seen and heard. Then he remembered Action Agency Memo 523, and in a sudden flash of inspiration realized who the Agent was.

Who is Codename Snowstorm?

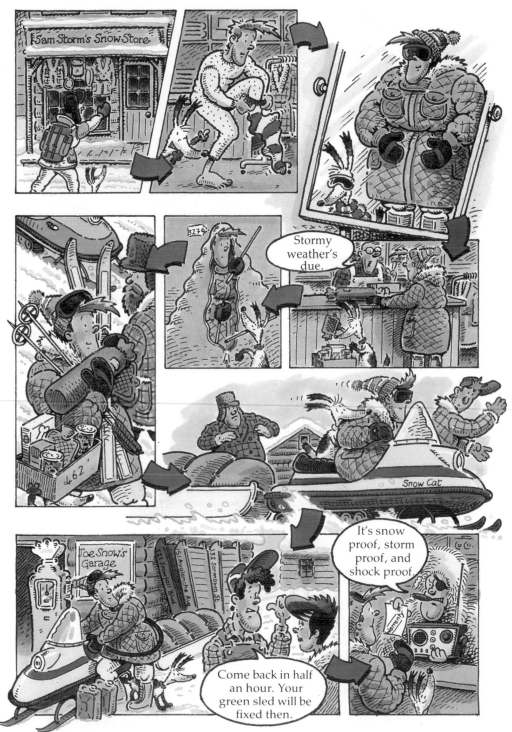

23

Into the Arctic

Arthur and Sleuth skidooed back to the garage where Snowstorm was collecting her sled. Arthur stepped forwards and flashed his Action Agency ID. Sleuth wagged his tail as Snowstorm gave the correct Action Agent's reply.

"Search, solve and survive," she whispered. "My name's Zoe, what's going on?"

Zoe listened intently while Arthur explained. As soon as he had finished, Zoe introduced Sleuth to her huskies, hitched up the sled and jumped aboard.

"Follow me," she yelled. "It's a long trek, but I know the way."

They sped off in a cloud of snow. Zoe led the others at breakneck speed over the bleak tundra. She used her natural instincts to guide them deeper and deeper into the freezing wastes, while steering clear of icy hazards and wild animals.

When night fell they set up camp and tried to thaw out by the fire. But it was a sleepless night, and by dawn they were back on the trail. Struggling against exhaustion, they raced over the snow until at last Zoe stopped and pointed to a cabin below. This was Caribou Creek.

24

25

The Cabin at Caribou Creek

Sleuth bounded on ahead to sniff out any trouble in the log cabin. He wagged his tail and barked the all-clear to the two agents. Arthur parked the skidoo while Zoe tied up her huskies, then they stepped inside. They glanced around Agent Alex's tidy cabin. Where was the map and the information hidden? The trio began searching.

"With our highly trained Agency skills, this won't take long," Arthur thought confidently.

Just then Zoe cried out. She was holding a large folder. Arthur dashed over and stared at the contents – Action Agency files and papers. They were important, but where was the map that Agent Alex had mentioned?

Agent Angus
special surviv
hang-gliding

Jane Printz
recent recruit –
ace photographer
– currently working
undercover
Thailand

Captain Jack
Tar
special skills –
surviving stormy seas
latest mission – North Sea
oil rig fire-fighting –
patrol commander

desert

AGENCY
SIGNALS
All signals use
basic equipment
that is readily
available :-
AIR TO GROUND
3 flashes
RED - GREEN - RED =
We will land

GROUND TO AIR
3 flashes
BLUE - GREEN - BLUE =
It's safe to land and
pick us up

SEA TO AIR
GREEN flash =
Make for safety

SEA TO SEA
2 RED flashes = DANGER

1 Arctic HQ
352 khz

2 Office
96 fm

3 Pacific HQ
108 long wave

4 Desert base
being repaired

5 Island base
35 fm

6 Jungle hut
373 khz

Zoe and Arthur carried on looking until they slumped dejectedly to the floor.

"Leave that lemming alone," Arthur suddenly shouted to Sleuth. "Or you'll . . ."

Too late. Sleuth crashed into the stove, sending logs flying. One of the logs bounced on the floor and split open. Out rolled a piece of paper.

"It's a Spider Organization map," shouted Zoe. "But what use is it?"

Arthur suddenly remembered the directions he had found in the canning factory. If they followed those directions using this map, he was sure they would locate the Spider Organization's secret Arctic base.

Where is Ice Station Spider?

Skidoo Sabotage

Just then Arthur heard a noise outside. He glanced out of the window and gasped. Armed villains were arriving. It was time to leave, and fast.

Zoe sprang into action as the door opened. She pulled it to, rammed the bolts home then grabbed the map and files.

There was no time to dive for cover as the Spider men opened fire. Bullets whistled through the door into the cabin.

"Our only chance is to stick together and make a break before we're trapped," Arthur shouted. "Follow me."

They dashed out of the back door. Zoe's sled was surrounded. They had to abandon it and sprint for the skidoo.

"All aboard," cried Arthur as the engine roared into life. "Hold on tight, let's go."

The skidoo hurtled away over the snows. Arthur turned to watch the villains disappearing in the distance. He didn't spot the snow drift looming ahead!

It's a bomb.

The Spider Organization's three favourite bombs.

◀ Bomb A
To defuse bomb, disconnect wire joining two of the green terminals.

Bomb B ▶
To make bomb safe, cut the wires connecting the green terminals to each other.

◀ Bomb C
Defuse bomb by cutting wire that connects a green to a yellow terminal.

Zoe managed to throw herself clear as Arthur and Sleuth were catapulted head first into the powdery snow. Zoe got groggily to her feet. She began making her way towards the muffled cries for help when something on the chassis of the upturned skidoo caught her eye.

She gasped in horror. It was a bomb! So that was why the villains had let them escape.

"Take cover," mumbled Arthur, burrowing deeper into the snow.

"But we must save the skidoo. It's all we have left since those villains captured my huskies and sled," sniffed Zoe.

She opened her Action Agency Handbook. First she must identify the bomb, then defuse it.

Can you defuse the bomb?

White-out

oe held her breath as she cut the wire. The bomb stopped ticking. She let out a huge sigh of relief and stowed the bomb in her pack. Arthur dug himself out of the snow drift and checked their essential survival equipment. The everything-proof unbreakable radio was broken! Arthur assessed their situation.

"There's a direct route to Ice Station Spider," Zoe said, once he had finished. "But it will be a long hard journey across the bleak Arctic wastes. We must start straight away."

Zoe was right. Arthur snapped on his snow goggles. He started the skidoo and the trio headed off. As they drove into the empty white landscape, Arthur shivered. Would they ever see Hudlum Bay again?

For four days and nights they struggled on, pitting their wits and Action Agency skills against the treacherous terrain and hostile climate. Biting winds froze their flesh. The trio stretched their limbs to breaking point as they hauled themselves over icy obstacles and escaped from angry Arctic animals.

At the end of the fifth day, they set up camp on the icecap. Zoe studied the map. They had made good progress Northwards, now maybe it was time to head East. While Zoe was checking their position, Arthur peered out of the tent and spotted some wreckage in the distance.

"I'll investigate that crashed chopper due West," Arthur said, trying to stop his teeth chattering. "Come on, Sleuth."

Be careful. I think there's a storm brewing.

Sleuth reluctantly trailed after Arthur. The wind blew away Zoe's warning. Arthur and Sleuth trudged on and on in a straight line towards the helicopter. The wind started howling and thick snow swirled around them.

"We must get back to the tent," Arthur shouted as gusts of wind blasted towards them, driving blinding snow into their eyes. "We'll never survive this weather in the open."

But as they retraced their steps, the tent disappeared in the white-out conditions. Arthur huddled next to Sleuth for warmth. He tipped out his pockets and suddenly realized they had a chance to get back.

**What can Arthur use?
How can they get back?**

Glacier Crossing

Arthur and Sleuth had thawed out by dawn when Zoe struck camp. They headed East and glided along smoothly until the skidoo shuddered, spluttered and died. They were out of petrol.

"It doesn't matter," said Zoe, pointing down. "We've made it to the Fox's Glacier, but this is where the going gets really tough. From now on we must go by foot. We'll only take what we can carry."

Sadly they abandoned the skidoo and sorted through their gear. Arthur staggered under the weight of his backpack, then he gritted his teeth and stared down defiantly.

They had to cross the glacier, despite the deadly crevasses, wild animals and thin ice.

Can you find a safe route across the glacier?

Ice Station Spider

The gentle slope on the other side of the glacier soon became an uphill struggle. Numb with cold, the trio scrabbled for a grip on the slippery ice.

At last they reached the top. Zoe peered through the mist. Ice Station Spider was somewhere in the valley below. They must get down for a closer look, but how?

Suddenly an ominous crack broke the silence and the ground collapsed from under them. Arthur, Zoe and Sleuth bounced and rolled down onto solid pack ice. Their equipment avalanched down the slope and landed around them.

Arthur could hardly believe his eyes. The base was right in front of them! They dived for cover as Zoe heard a high-pitched whining noise, but it wasn't an alarm. The radio had fixed itself. Zoe contacted the Action Agency and listened for orders.

SIGNAL EQUIPMENT

"Getting in should be easy," said Arthur confidently. "That fence will never stop highly trained Action Agents like us."

"That's no ordinary fence," replied Zoe. "It's electric, and carrying a lethal load."

Arthur gulped. How would they get past the killer fence? Just then Sleuth chased off after an Arctic fox. Arthur sighed. This was no time for games. He began studying the equipment nearby.

How can they get into the base?

Arthur and Zoe squeezed after Sleuth. Zoe held the torch while Arthur enlarged the tunnel with an ice pick. It was slow work, but at last they crawled up to the surface and wriggled out. They were inside the base.

Just then a searchlight swept over the ground towards them. Zoe dived back into the tunnel as Arthur and Sleuth flattened themselves face down into the snow. The searchlight passed silently over them.

Action Agents here! Go and guard the hostages, you three come with me.

Boss, we've found a tunnel leading into the base, with an Action Agency Handbook in it.

While Zoe was planting the 'diversion', Arthur and Sleuth watched Bella lock away the last deadly germ bomb. The safe door had just clanged shut when a mean-looking guard rushed into the hut shouting.

Arthur gasped. The tunnel had been discovered, but what about Zoe? Bella Donna punched an alarm button on the desk and barked orders to her henchmen. A siren began to wail as the crooks raced out of the hut.

The agents leapt into action. Keeping to the shadows, they darted through the camp, checking buildings and dodging guards. They peered in through the windows of two adjacent huts and grinned triumphantly.

At last they had found the germ bombs and the hostages. First they must get the bombs.

"We need a diversion," said Zoe smiling. "And I've got just the thing."

Arthur broke into the hut and raced over to the safe. It would be easy to open, he knew the key word. But the console buttons were numbered! How could he tap in letters? Just then Zoe appeared beside him.

She began checking the papers on the desk and the walls. Arthur joined her. Maybe they contained a clue. It was a long shot, but they had to take it.

How can they open the safe?

Rescue

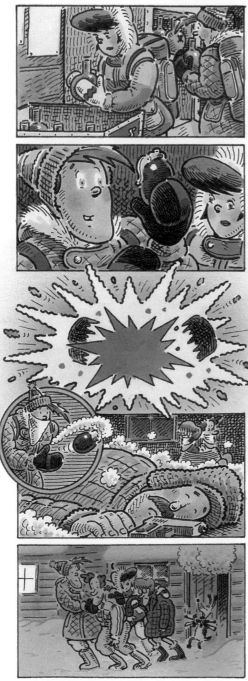

The safe door swung open. Trying to stop their hands shaking, Arthur and Zoe began gingerly picking up the phials containing the deadly germs and placing them gently in a steel box. At last the safe was empty. Now they must release the hostages, but what about their guards?

"I've got something up my sleeve for them," whispered Arthur, producing a knockout gas grenade. "It's quick-working and has no lasting side effects."

"Great idea," said Zoe, as they crept outside. "But what's happened to my diversion."

Just then an enormous BANG echoed through the camp. Zoe smiled. That should keep the villains busy.

Arthur tried the door to the hostage hut. It was unlocked. He and Zoe tied scarves round their faces then Arthur lobbed the grenade into the hut.

Five seconds later the Action Agents followed. They were just in time to see the guards slump to the floor, asleep. Sleuth disarmed them while Zoe and Arthur untied the dopey hostages, hauled them out of the hut and locked the door behind them.

Agent Alex and Professor Tube soon came to in the cold. They stared around in amazement. Ice Station Spider was in chaos. The fuel dump was ablaze and gang members were racing around trying to put out the fire. They were too busy to notice the agents and the freed hostages.

Suddenly Sleuth's ears pricked up. Above the roar of the flames he could hear an engine. He barked at the others and they stared upwards. Arthur spotted a dark shape hovering in the sky.

"It's an Agency helicopter," he shouted. "We're saved."

"But it's not landing," Zoe yelled.

Zoe was right, and Arthur suddenly realized why. The chopper needed landing signals. Arthur racked his brains. He knew where to get the signals, but what were the correct ones?

Where can Arthur find signals? Which ones should he use?

No Escape?

Arthur ducked under the rotor blades and jumped into the helicopter, seconds before it roared up into the sky.

"Mission accomplished," Arthur yelled as he saw the germ bombs and everyone safely aboard.

"Not yet," boomed a familiar voice from the cockpit.

Arthur gasped as the pilot turned round, smiling. It was Uncle Jake!

SIGNAL EQUIPMENT

ESCAPE ROUTES
TO BE COVERED

Gate 1 —
Gate 2 —
Gate 3 —
Rocket —
Helicopter —
Skidoos —
Any other way out ?

"Detachments of back-up agents have landed to round up the villains," he said, handing Arthur a piece of paper. "As you know the situation on the ground, I want you to check that we've covered all possible escape routes out of the base."

Arthur stared at the list and peered down at the chaotic scene below. The Agency seemed to have all the routes covered.

Have they?

Back at the Office

But remember that we must never relax our efforts to solve mysteries and to defeat the Spider Organization.

Arthur was proudly clutching the Agency's highest award, the Action Arrow, presented by Uncle Jake. Arthur looked round happily at the familiar faces.

As he listened to Uncle Jake's speech his mind flashed back to the Arctic operation against Ice Station Spider. The back-up agents had found the tunnel in time to catch all the villains.

Except one. Bella Donna had managed to slip through their fingers. Suddenly Arthur's spine tingled. He sensed that someone was watching, and he had a feeling he knew who it was. This time there would be no escape. Arthur tensed himself, ready to spring into action . . .

Who's watching Arthur?

Clues

You will need to hold this page in front of a mirror to read the clues.

Pages 4-5

Look back to the Action Code on page 3. A = §   B = Π

Pages 6-7

What did Agent Alex say? Look closely at the town plan.

Pages 8-9

Think carefully about the woman's reply.

Pages 10-11

This is easy. Use your eyes.

Pages 12-13

Compare the figures that look like Bella with the real Bella on pages 10-11.

Pages 14-15

Where is the word "in" in relation to the word "out".

Pages 16-17

This is easy. Check the characters that appear earlier in the book.

Pages 18-19

There are two different codes. Try thinking backwards for one and swapping the first and last letters of each word for the other.

Pages 20-21

This is easy.

Pages 22-23

Decode Memo 523 on page 3.

Pages 26-27

Look back to the coded directions on page 19.

Pages 28-29

Look carefully at the electrical circuits for each bomb in the Handbook. Which one matches the bomb on the skidoo?

Pages 30-31

Arthur set off in a straight line due West away from the tent. In what direction must they travel to get back to it?

Pages 32-33

You don't need a clue for this.

Pages 34-35

Is there a way under the fence?

Pages 36-37

Look closely at all the pieces of paper on the walls and on the desk. One of them has the first four letters of the key word written on it.

Pages 38-39

Look at the Agency Signals on page 26, and check the buildings in the base on pages 34-35.

Pages 40-41

How did Arthur get into the base?

Page 42

This is easy. Use your eyes.

Answers

Pages 4-5

The message is written in Action Code. This is what it says:

PROCEED TO POST OFFICE. ANSWER GREEN PHONE. CONTACT WILL ASK IS THE BAKED ALASKA READY. REPLY YES IT WILL BE RIGHT ON TIME. AGENCY KIT IN LOCKER 13. KEY UNDER LETTUCE.

Pages 6-7

Arthur should go to the safe house.

The safe house is here.

It is the only house with the landing flight path directly overhead and a fountain in a park to the South East.

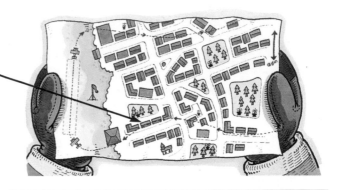

Pages 8-9

Arthur thinks logically about the woman's reply and realizes that she is lying. If she knew he had rung twice, either she had heard the first ring, or someone must have told her. Arthur also spots a face at the upstairs window.

Pages 10-11

Bella has dropped this piece of paper.

Pages 12-13

This is the real Bella Donna. The others are all wearing slightly different clothes.

No hood.

Wrong grip on boots.

Different colour jacket.

Different colour boots.

Pages 14-15

Arthur notices that the word "in" is written on its side, and that it is also inside the middle letter of the word "out".

Thinking laterally, he realizes that the password is 'Inside Out'.

Pages 16-17

Arthur recognizes four people from the town square on pages 12-13.

Pages 18-19

The code on the piece of paper with the Spider logo can be deciphered by swapping the first and last letters of each word. This is what it says with punctuation added:

YOU CAN'T FLY DIRECTLY TO BASE DUE TO MOUNTAINS AND SNOWSTORMS. YOU MUST FOLLOW THE SPIDER ROUTE. FLY NORTH TO FIRST BEACON THEN TURN EAST TO THE SEA. CARIBOU CREEK IS DUE WEST. CONTINUE NORTH TO SECOND BEACON. BELOW BEACON IS A VILLAGE. AT THE VILLAGE FLY WEST THROUGH VALLEY TO THIRD BEACON, THEN SOUTH TOWARDS BEACON NUMBER FOUR. BELOW BEACON IS A GLACIER. FOLLOW THE GLACIER NW TOWARDS THE FIFTH BEACON. THE BASE IS IN THE VALLEY ON THE EAST SIDE OF THE MOUNTAIN SE OF THE LAST BEACON.

Pages 18-19 (continued)

Each paragraph on the pink pad of paper has been written backwards with spaces inserted irregularly between letters. This is what it says:

SPIDER ORGANIZATION WORLD DOMINATION PLAN 3.

PHASE 1. BELLA DONNA AND THE TRAPPER GANG TO BUILD SECRET BASE IN REMOTE PART OF ARCTIC. BASE TO BE CALLED ICE STATION SPIDER. COMPLETED.

PHASE 2. BELLA TO KIDNAP SCIENTIST PROFESSOR TESS TUBE AND FORCE HER TO WORK AT ICE STATION SPIDER. ENGINEERS TO CONSTRUCT SPIDER ROCKET. COMPLETED.

PHASE 3. PROFESSOR TUBE WILL MAKE LETHAL GERM BOMBS FOR OUR ROCKET. BELLA TO WIND UP ACTIVITIES IN HUDLUM BAY THEN RETURN TO GUARD ICE STATION SPIDER. ONCE THE BOMBS ARE FINISHED WE WILL HOLD THE WORLD TO RANSOM AND DEMAND TOTAL GLOBAL CONTROL.

Pages 20-21

This is the only place where Arthur and Sleuth can hide.

Pages 22-23

This is Codename Snowstorm.

Come back in half an hour. Your green sled will be fixed then.

Arthur works this out by thinking back to Action Agency Memo 523 on page 3. When decoded it says:

WHEN WRITTEN, ALL AGENTS' CODENAMES MUST APPEAR AS ANAGRAMS WITH NUMBERS IN REVERSE ORDER.

Arthur realizes that the address written on the side of the green sled is an anagram of Snowstorm, and that 132 is Snowstorm's number written backwards.

The owner of the green sled must be Codename Snowstorm. When Arthur overhears the mechanic he realizes who the sled's owner is.

Pages 26-27

Arthur remembers the directions he decoded on page 19.

He follows them on the map. The route is marked in black.

Ice Station Spider is here.

Caribou Creek is here.

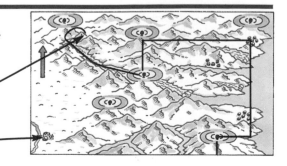

Pages 28-29

The bomb planted on the skidoo has the same electrical circuit as Bomb C in the Handbook. To defuse it, Zoe must cut this wire.

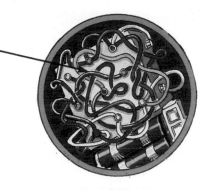

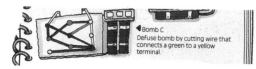

◄ Bomb C
Defuse bomb by cutting wire that connects a green to a yellow terminal.

Pages 30-31

Arthur and Sleuth set off from the tent, walking in a straight line towards the crashed chopper. Before they reach it, they are forced to turn back and begin to retrace their steps before stopping.

They walked due West towards the chopper, so Arthur realizes they must head due East to get back to the tent. To plot this course, Arthur must use the compass he has turned out of his pocket.

Pages 32-33

The safe route across the glacier is marked in black.

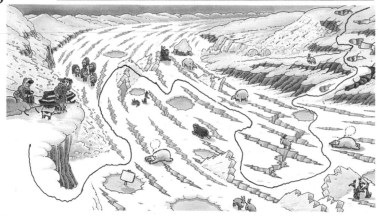

Pages 34-35

There is a tunnel that leads under the fence and into the base. This is Arthur's way in.

When Sleuth chases after the Arctic fox he enters the tunnel here.

The Arctic fox is running out of the tunnel here.

This piece of paper shows the first four letters of the key word with numbers written below them.

Arthur realizes that each letter in the alphabet is represented by a different number. He also suspects that there is a pattern to the code.

He knows from the paper that A = 12, so he continues this pattern where B = 13, C = 14 and so on until O = 26. When he reaches P, he goes back to number 1 then continues Q = 2, R = 3, S = 4, T = 5 and on until he reaches Z. This fits in with the letters and numbers on the piece of paper

Arthur then reads off the numbers that represent each letter of the key word 'TARANTULA'.

To open the safe he punches in these numbers: 5, 12, 3, 12, 25, 5, 6, 23, 12.

Pages 38-39

Arthur can find signalling equipment in the hut right beside him.

These are the correct Agency signals.

Zoe found them in Agent Alex's log cabin on page 26.

Pages 40-41 — Page 42

The Action Agency haven't covered the tunnel that Arthur and Zoe used to enter the base.

Bella Donna is watching from the window. ➙

You can also spot some familiar faces from Arthur's earlier adventures.